Valentine's Arrow

Holidays After Dark

Astrid Vail

Rogue Queen Publishing

Valentine's Arrow

Copyright © 2023 by Astrid Vail & Rogue Queen Publishing

All rights reserved. No part of this book may be used or reproduced, stored or transmitted in any form or by any means, electronic, mechanical, photocopying, recording, scanning, or otherwise in any manner whatsoever without written permission except in the case of brief quotations bodied in critical articles or reviews.

It is illegal to copy this book, post it on a website, or distribute it by any means without permission.

This book is a work of fiction. Names, characters, businesses, organizations, places, events, and incidents either are the product of the author's imagination or are used fictitiously. Any resemblance to actual persons, living or dead, events, or locales is entirely coincidental.

Cover Art by www.getcovers.com

Edited by www.nicegirlnaughtyedits.com

ISBN:

eBook: 978-1-958641-04-0

Paperback: 978-1-958641-08-8

First Edition: February 2023

Content Warning: Contains graphic sex scenes and adult language.

Contents

Blurb & Content Warning	IV
1. Chapter One	1
2. Chapter Two	6
3. Chapter Three	12
4. Chapter Four	17
5. Chapter Five	24
6. Chapter Six	29
7. Chapter Seven	34
Also by Astrid Vail	40
About Astrid Vail	42

Blurb & Content Warning

After losing her job and relationship in one fell swoop, Arrow stumbles across a listing requesting help to plan a Valentine's Day bash.

Only there is one problem.

The address listed is in the Night City, a place full of demons, shifters, and everything in between. A place no respectable fairy such as herself should wander into.

But the Night City is not what it seems and one little mishap later, Arrow finds herself face to face with the most gorgeous man she has ever seen.

Now Arrow can't help but wonder...

Could the Night City and the man she finds herself instantly enamored with be the new beginning she needs?

Valentine's Arrow is a short M/F paranormal erotica that includes graphic sex scenes and adult language.

Chapter One

"WHAT DO YOU MEAN, terminated?" Arrow yelled, her voice hitting a shrill pitch.

The Grand Mistress of Fairies Grace looked down her nose at Arrow. "This institute does not tolerate lawless behavior in any manner. We do not employ anyone with a record."

Arrow's mouth dropped wide. "You, you, you have got to be kidding me! All I did was glue his wings together. He was the one who—"

The Grand Mistress held up her hand. "Enough. You held a temp position to begin with. You can return to the job agency and find another job. Now get off the property."

Arrow snapped her mouth shut and floated back down to the ground. In her anger and disbelief, her iridescent wings had gone into hyper speed, pulling Arrow a few inches off the ground. She turned and stomped out of the hallway, through the imposing open doors of the college, and launched herself off the stately steps into the sky.

The angry buzz of her wings kept the few other fairies flying around out of her path, and soon Arrow found herself in front of the temp agency. She landed in line and waited; the angry tap of her foot drowning out the surrounding whispers. The sun beat down on her head and shoulders relentlessly, and Arrow wished she had the foresight to have grabbed a light jacket.

And hat.

And sunglasses.

She sighed in defeat as the line moved up one person before immediately stopping. Arrow pushed at her short, dark brown hair. It was straightened into a stylish shoulder-length bob, but she sorely missed her long hair. Her hair naturally fell in curling locks, and she missed the way it used to bounce when it was up in a ponytail. Her defeated look turned to a grimace. Anger blossomed under her breastbone, and she glanced down at her hands.

Nails, usually long and manicured, were now cut to the quick, pink nail polish chipping.

"Whatever," Arrow murmured. "He deserved a destroyed apartment. What's a few broken nails?"

The satyr in front of Arrow glanced over his shoulder before dismissing her words and going back to staring at the phone in his hand. Clearly, Arrow was muttering to herself. They moved forward, another person in line, and she quickly lost herself in thought.

A few hours later, Arrow found herself seated in front of a pissed off looking elf. The elf sighed and slammed the file down on the desk. "No jobs will hire you until you do your community service."

Arrow threw her hands in the air. "It's not like I murdered anyone. *I* should be the one pressing charges. I mean, do you see what he did to my hair?" Arrow picked at the ends of her bob for emphasis, but the elf had no sympathy for her.

"Not my problem."

Arrow sulked in her chair and crossed her arms. "I'm not moving until you find me a job. There must be something."

The elf pursed his lips and shook his head before sliding a paper her way. "Here is a listing of community service opportunities. Come back once you complete your hours and we will see what is available."

She wanted to sulk longer, but the elf gave her a dismissing look before yelling out *next,* and Arrow slid off her chair in a daze. She wandered over to the massive doors, anger lifting her into the air. An older looking parchment caught her eye as she buzzed by the overflowing clipboard posting about upcoming events. She ripped it off the board quickly before buzzing away into the bright sunlit outdoors. A bench sitting empty on the perfectly manicured grass beckoned and Arrow landed on it. She uncrumpled the paper in her hand and read, hope slowly tumbling away.

Assistant Event Planner Wanted
Valentine's Day Bash
Come walk on the wild side and plan the party of a lifetime.
Call 876-4567

Arrow sighed. It was dated in the corner, for two years ago. Not only that, but the address printed in fine print below listed the Dark City. A place she had only heard horror stories about. A place where certain beings roamed, and where the sun only shined a few hours a day. A city where night ruled supreme. All sorts of wickedness came from the Dark City.

Arrow worried at her bottom lip. She briefly wondered if the party ever happened. And why had they advertised for it here? In Fairy City, of all places.

VALENTINE'S ARROW

The sound of a voice snapped Arrow back to the present, and she scowled. Across the grassy courtyard stood her ex and his gaggle of friends. A pretty fairy, scantily clad in a light green flowing gown, with long curly blonde hair clung to his arm. Arrow cursed silently and clutched at the ends of her short hair. She wouldn't have been in this mess in the first place if her ex and friends hadn't gotten drunk and set her hair on fire. Then he had the nerve to cheat on her because he didn't think she was pretty without her long hair. His cruel words had pushed Arrow over the edge. In retaliation, she glued the bastard's wings together and destroyed his small apartment.

She watched them saunter away, and Arrow's chest grew heavy, sadness smothering her rage. With a deep breath, she pulled out her phone and dialed the number on the paper. It rang twice before rolling over to a voice mail. It stated little, just a curt 'leave a message.'

Arrow hung up quickly and shoved the paper into her purse. She was insane to have even called the number. And what if someone actually picked up? The Dark City was no place for her. Arrow instead took out the other piece of paper listing all the potential places for her to do community service.

With a disappointed sigh, she called the first number.

Chapter Two

Arrow had lost her little fairy mind. It was the only excuse she could come up with as she landed on the dark cobblestone sidewalk. She glanced at the time on her phone and worried at her lip. Currently, she was supposed to be doing her first act of community service, digging trenches out in the garden district. Instead, she was in the Dark City, in front of a closed building, with dusk rapidly encroaching.

To be fair, it was only ten a.m., but the Dark City only got four hours of sunshine a day. Arrow pulled at her form fitted pink halter top, making sure it

VALENTINE'S ARROW

was tucked into her black jean shorts. Her matching pink work boots thudded against the cobblestones as she approached the door and knocked. The door didn't budge when she tried to open it. She leaned into the window and cupped her hands. It looked barren. Arrow squinted when she saw a shadow move and knocked on the window.

She waited a moment before taking a step away with a sigh. It was just a trick of the eye. Turning on her heel, ready to take flight, Arrow hesitated as the sound of a deadbolt being thrown caught her attention. She turned back around with a smile plastered on her face as the door slammed open.

It caught her right in the forehead, and she stumbled back in shock. Pain exploded through her head and neck, and she slowly lifted her fingers. They came away tinged with blood. Arrow's heart raced, breath coming out in short bursts as she tilted to the side, and everything went dark.

***

"Oh no, no, no, no, no... I killed a fairy... I killed a fairy." Incessant muttering brought Arrow back to consciousness slowly. The low growl and sin-laden voice of a man had her eyes open instantly.

"You didn't kill her, Desi. Stop worrying."

Arrow shot upright into a sitting position before grabbing her head. A dull throb radiated through her skull, her neck stiff. "Ouch," she whined, before getting a good look at the two people standing in front of her. They both had the same silvered gray complexion and dark starry eyes.

The woman gave Arrow a look of pure relief, her fidgeting hands pulling at her long, dark black hair. She was tall and lithe in stature and all but danced around the living room Arrow was in. But it was the man who caught Arrow's attention the most. His dark black hair was cut short on the sides, though longer on the top in a style Arrow could only describe as dangerous yet fashionable. His face masculine and handsome. A small smile tugged at the corner of his full lips, and he settled back into the chair he was lounging in. Arrow realized she was staring, her mouth slightly ajar, and the man winked at her.

"See, Desi, she is fine. Aren't you, Princess?"

Arrow blinked rapidly and flinched back as the woman, Desi, rounded the couch quickly and snatched Arrow's hands in hers. "I'm so sorry. You were close to the door, and it sticks. I just kicked it open, and... and... and why were you even at the door?"

Arrow was still reeling from being called princess by the sinfully handsome man who looked like he emerged from the night sky itself. It took her a moment to catch up with what Desi was rambling about. Though apparently not fast enough. Desi's face fell into panic once again.

"Val," she whined. "I think I gave her brain damage. Why isn't she speaking?" Desi turned back to Arrow. "Why aren't you speaking? Can you speak?"

"I'm sure she can speak, Desi. Just let her process."

Val's voice slid down Arrow's spine like living smoke, rubbing at her in ways she never knew a voice could. She was equal parts scared and aroused. "I can speak," Arrow whispered. "Can I have some water?"

Desi flew off the couch, launching into the kitchen with a loud clatter. Arrow winced at the banging of cabinets, and Val frowned slightly, his luscious lips tilting to the side. Desi was back on the couch moments later, water sloshing over her hands as it spilled from the glass. She carefully took it from Desi and sipped. The water cooled her parched throat even though it did nothing for the heat rising in her cheeks. Val was still looking at her and just his presence was getting Arrow hot and bothered.

Before her brain short-circuited and she did something deliciously wicked to him, Arrow turned her attention back to Desi. Pulling the piece of paper from her pocket, she handed it over.

"I know it's two years too late, but Valentine's Day is right around the corner and I, ummm... I know it's silly, but..."

Arrow trailed off as Desi stared at the paper in her hand. "Oh," she breathed before glancing over her shoulder at Val. He titled his head and gave Desi a curt nod. She turned back to Arrow, a large smile encompassing her face. "Are you offering to help with event planning?"

Arrow gave Desi a hesitant smile. "If you need the help still, I would love to be of service."

Desi jumped off the couch with a holler and began all but running around the room. "Yes! This will be amazing. This year will be so magical with a real fairy here!"

She zipped across the room, hugging Val before rushing over to Arrow and pulling her into a tight squeeze. The hug only lasted a moment before Desi zipped away, disappearing into the hallway only to return with a large planner in her hands. She slammed it onto the couch before Val interrupted her excitement with a cough. "Before you get too preoccupied, Desi. Don't you have a shift at the bakery?"

Desi blinked rapidly before a sheepish look crossed over her face. "Shoot, I do. I guess..." She glanced over at Arrow. "I guess you could leave your number and I'll call you?"

Arrow reached out, patting Desi on the leg. "Of course."

Desi grinned and ran out of the living room. Her goodbye echoed out as a door slammed and Arrow blushed, realizing she was now completely alone with Val.

And he was staring at her.

Chapter Three

VAL LEANED FORWARD AND lifted a finger to stroke his bottom lip. Arrow clenched her thighs together and clamped down the low moan in her throat that threatened to escape. Val was too attractive to be real. When the door hit her in the head, she really must have suffered brain damage.

Arrow peeled her gaze away from the way Val was stroking his lip, mind lost in thought, and instead reached up to prod at her forehead. It was a little tender still, but nothing to be concerned about. She was a fast healer, all fairies were. Arrow glanced back at Val and her breath caught. Before his gaze had been glazed over in thought, but now it was focused, and he was staring at Arrow like she was prey. His eyes followed her hand as she slowly lowered it back down to her lap. Then they dipped lower, taking in her bare legs. A smirk touched the edges of his mouth when he got to her pink work boots. A strangled noise echoed through the room and his eyes darted back up to Arrow's face.

She desperately pretended the strangled noise did not just come from her and glanced everywhere but at Val. She caught sight of an oval mirror high on the wall and jumped to her feet, wings moving vigorously to bring her up to the mirror's height. Arrow gasped at the sight of her tangled hair. Not to mention, there were smudges on her shoulders and arms. She could only assume it was grime from the cobblestones. Quickly, Arrow began running her fingers through her hair to untangle the mess. "I can't believe I look so terrible. I must look like a—"

A low rumbling growl caught Arrow off guard, and she turned slowly, hands paused in her hair. Val was standing right behind her, and her wings missed a beat, pausing for a moment. His hands shot out immediately, an arm wrapping around her waist while his other hand grabbed her upper thigh. Within a mere breath, Arrow was pressed against Val's chest. She grabbed his broad shoulders on instinct and her eyes widened as the look of bliss passed over his face before snapping back to neutral.

"Are you okay, Princess? I didn't mean to startle you."

Arrow shook her head and licked her suddenly parched lips. Val's eyes dipped and this time Arrow felt *and* heard a rumble come from his chest. "Are you purring?" She whispered before sliding a hand to his chest.

The rumbled deepened and Val rasped, ignoring her question. "I should put you down before I do something stupid."

"Like?" Arrow's voice cracked, lips going slightly ajar in shock at her own boldness.

Val's eyes hooded, hand from her thigh releasing and making its way up her side. His fingers lingered along her collarbone, before cupping her jaw. Arrow wrapped her legs around Val's waist, barely able to lock her ankles. He was so big compared to her, and an involuntary moan slipped from her lips. Her moan elicited a groan from Val as he wrapped his large hand around the back of her neck and captured her lips with his own. The kiss scorched Arrow down to her core, the fabric of her entire being lighting up with flames of desire.

Val pulled away and Arrow fisted his shirt in her hands. She jerked him back in, lips colliding once more. She parted her lips as his tongue demanded entrance to her mouth. As the most intense kiss of her life ensued, Arrow tugged at Val's shirt. She heard the buttons littering the ground over the rumbling in his chest. He fisted her hair and broke the kiss, to Arrow's dismay. His breathing was heavy, and he looked as distraught as Arrow felt.

"Something stupid like that," Val murmured, and she felt heat rush to her face.

"Oh," Arrow murmured as she unlocked her legs and tried to push away. Embarrassment flooded her veins and Arrow ducked her head, hiding her face with her hair.

Val tightened his arm around her waist with a grunt. "Princess, that came out wrong." Arrow peeked at Val's face through her hair and worried at her lip, taking in the crease between his eyebrows. Val sucked in a deep breath before continuing, "An hour ago, my sister knocked you out with a door. I just want to make sure you are okay before making any moves on you." He chuckled and added, "I don't even know your name."

Relief flooded her veins, and she gave Val a bright smile before scrunching her nose and rubbing at her forehead. It was still tender, but overall, Arrow felt fine. A low groan encompassed the room, and she met Val's eyes.

"Fuck, Princess," he murmured, and Arrow felt his chest hitch, the purring taking on a deeper cadence. He reached up, stroking the bridge of her nose lightly. "You are unbelievably adorable."

Arrow warmed at his words and the look he was giving her. She grabbed his hand and lowered it to her mouth. Nipping at his fingertips, she glanced at Val through her eyelashes, the tips of her lips hitching at the sides, when he groaned. "I would feel better if you kissed me again. And my name is Arrow."

The hand she was holding slipped from hers as Val cupped the back of her neck, fingers lacing into her hair. He pulled her close, lips scrapping against hers. "Arrow," Val whispered, and she blushed at the way seductive way he said her name before kissing her again.

Chapter Four

SHE SANK INTO THE kiss, barely registering Val move nor her knees brushing against the couch. Val released her waist and his fingers trailed lightly across the bare strip of her skin between the top of her shorts and the hem of her shirt. Arrow whimpered at the touch, rubbing her front against his chest. She released her hold on his shoulders and pulled at the laces holding her shirt on. She didn't care if they were going too fast or if she was temporarily insane for wanting to get down and dirty with this relative stranger.

All she could think about was how good his bare skin would feel against her own. Val seemed to have the same idea as he shrugged the rest of his shirt off and threw it to the floor, along with hers. "Princess," he murmured as he placed his hand back on her. The one on the back of her neck tightened slightly. Arrow whimpered and rubbed against him. He pulled back slightly and nipped at her bottom lip.

Arrow gasped as he continued nipping at her lips before trailing kisses across her jawline and down her neck. Her wings fluttered as she felt pleasure building deep inside of her, straining for release. Arrow sank her hands in Val's hair, trying to pull him away before she did something silly like orgasm from just a few kisses.

Val lifted his head with a sly look encompassing his face and licked her neck, making his way back up her jawline to nip at her ear. Arrow's eyes rolled and her back arched as Val's fingers trailed up her spine. He dragged a finger across the edge of her gossamer wings and Arrow came undone, her pussy clenching tightly. Her breathless scream was obscured by Val's soft chuckle, and he kissed her lightly on the lips.

She opened her eyes with a groan, about to ask Val why he stopped, but the words dried up on her tongue. A fine misting of pink dust coated the couch and Val's arms and chest. Arrow's cheeks warmed in embarrassment. Never had she orgasmed so hard that fairy dust exploded from her wings. And here it was, coating them both. She shook her head, about to apologize, when Val caressed her jaw and rumbled, "Does it change colors with every orgasm?"

Her jaw dropped and Arrow choked on her words, "I... uh... I don't, umm... I don't know."

Val kissed her through the stammering sentence and lifted her off his lap. He spun her around, placing her on the top of the couch. Arrow gripped his shoulders tightly for balance as his hands tugged at her shorts. He pulled them off along with her very soaked panties. She didn't see where he threw them, concentrating solely on the look Val was giving her. His grin was wicked, and Arrow swore her pussy clenched with his next words. "We will find out together, Princess."

Val threw her legs over his shoulders and dipped his head. His hands grabbed tight on Arrow's waist, so she didn't careen backwards off the couch. Val licked at her inner thigh and blew softly. Arrow ran her hands through his hair as he nipped and licked at her legs. She harrumphed slightly at the sight of her pink work boots still on her feet. She wiggled, eliciting a groan from Val. "My boots are still on."

"I am aware, Princess. But they are just so damn cute, just like you. I don't want you to take them off."

Arrow rolled her eyes, about to protest that men like heels, not pink work boots, when Val growled and licked her pussy. Her hands jerked in his hair, back arching, and Arrow was pretty sure her eyes crossed. "Oh, sugar tits," she moaned as Val swirled his tongue along her clit before nipping at it gently.

"Sugar tits." He chuckled before giving her pussy another good lick. "That's adorable."

Arrow wanted to say something, anything to keep the banter going, but her breathing grew heavy as Val's tongue lavished her, slow and steady. She already felt the low pool of pleasure in her core growing, building like a dam ready to overflow. Her toes curled in her boots, wings vibrating so hard Arrow was worried they would break away and take flight on their own.

Soft meowing sounds filled the room, along with the heavy rumbling coming from Val's chest. Arrow barely registered the meowing sounds came from her as her hands tightened in Val's hair. The pool of pleasure in her core spilled over and Arrow cried out as she shuddered. Val gave her one last lick before allowing Arrow to melt like a puddle into his arms. She wrapped her shaking arms around his neck and rubbed her face against his bare chest. Fingers tickled over her back, running up and down her spine. "Gold," Val purred, and Arrow blinked a few times, still reeling from her orgasm high.

"Gold?" she whispered.

VALENTINE'S ARROW

Val's hands swept from her back to her head and into her hair, massaging at her scalp. "Gold," he purred again. "It does change colors. It's gold this time."

Arrow lifted her head and blushed. A fine mist of gold dust mingled over the pink, coating the couch, Val's chest, and shoulders. She bit her lip and pushed up to straddle Val's enormous frame and immense erection straining against her. With a grumble, she grabbed at the zipper of his pants. "I can't believe these are still on."

Val chuckled underneath her and tucked his arms under his head. Arrow rolled her eyes as she unzipped him, and his cock sprang out into her hands. Her eyes grew wide at the length and width, and for a fleeting moment, Arrow wondered if the massive thing would fit inside of her. She ran her hands down the length of his cock, marveling at it. Val's rumbling purr deepened at her touch and Arrow bit her lip. "Will it even fit?" she murmured.

Val groaned, hips jerking slightly as she squeezed him. "Princess, I promise you, I will fit."

He pulled at Arrow's hands, placing them on his shoulders as he sat up. Arrow had no choice but to move with him, straddling his lap. She was still so deliciously wet, and Val pulled her closer, hands gripped tight on her hips. Arrow wiggled and rubbed his cock against her entrance and clit. Her pussy tightened in anticipation of taking something so large inside of her. Val caught her mouth with his before positioning her hips and entrance over the head of his cock.

Arrow whimpered at the pressure as he slowly breached her entrance. He slid in an inch before pulling out. "Fuck, Princess. You're so tight," he whispered against her lips. He moved a hand from her waist to rub at her clit and Arrow groaned. She grabbed the back of his neck as Val slid inside again, this time a few inches farther. She knew he was going agonizingly slow so her pussy could accommodate his girth, but Arrow wanted him fully inside of her that instant.

As he pulled out and plunged back in slowly, Arrow felt Val loosen his other hand to grab her ass. Arrow took her freedom and slammed her hips down. She came, hard and fast, as his cock impaled her and cried out in absolute pleasure.

"Arrow!" Val roared, too little too late, cock twitching inside of her. He grabbed her hair, forehead aligning with hers, and growled, "You are a naughty fucking Princess. We were going slow for a reason."

She giggled against his lips, and he growled again, hand tightening in her hair. But instead of pulling back out, Val ground his hips in a circular motion, eliciting a small squeak of pleasure from Arrow. He continued his slow bump and grind, gripping Arrow in a way where she was trapped in his embrace. She held onto him, enjoying the ride.

Her eyes crossed, breathless moans and pleasure-ridden squeaks filling the room every time Val bottomed out inside of her. His grip tightened and Val groaned, head dropping into the crook of her neck as Arrow felt his cock pulsate inside of her. The after waves of desire rolled over Arrow, her pussy clenching against Val's cock as he slowly pulled out of her.

"Let's go to bed, Princess," he whispered in her ear and Arrow sighed as Val scooped her up. She snuggled into his chest and drifted off to sleep right there in his arms.

Chapter Five

A LOUD THUD PULLED Arrow from sleep, and she yawned against the hard, purring pillow under her head. Arrow blinked rapidly, and the pillow shifted under her.

"That tickles, Princess," Val rumbled and Arrow giggled. A soft sigh escaped her lips as his hand trailed up her spine and started massaging her neck. She sank into a blissful state of being, listening to Val's soft purring and barely registering the sound of footsteps echoing through the purrs.

"Val! Did the cute little fairy leave her number? Or did you scare her away with your drooling? And what is up with all this damn glitter?" The voice grew louder, footsteps landing right outside the door.

Arrow snapped her eyes open as Val's hand on her neck tightened. She turned her head in time to see the doorknob turn and squeaked in alarm. The door swung open, and Desi froze mid-stride, mouth hanging open in shock. Val's chest started shaking, a snort escaping as Desi shifted her gaze. A glowing hue surrounded her, and a loud snap echoed. Arrow scrambled off the bed in alarm.

In Desi's place, a large, obsidian dark panther now stood. It was the size of a small horse, with eyes glowing silver. Five tails dipped and swirled with invisible wind, serrated tail tips cutting into the door frame. Steam erupted from its snout and a low rumble echoed through the room. Arrow was still staring in disbelief as the pillow sailed across the room.

"Get out of here, Desi," Val grumbled. The monster in Desi's place turned and sauntered away. One tail snapped out and pulled the door shut with a loud thud. Arrow was still staring at the door as Val pulled her back into his embrace. She could hear her frantic inhales and could only imagine how wide her eyes looked. She was half convinced they were about to pop out of her head like a cartoon.

"You... you're... you... y..." Arrow stammered, teeth chattering.

Val sighed and leaned his head against the bed frame. "Yes. We are Hell Cats."

Arrow sucked in a loud breath and instantly clamped her hands over her mouth. A scream built in the back of her throat, and she had to fight to keep it down. "But... but... I thought Hell Cats..." Arrow stammered.

Val remained quiet, letting the silence build until it became apparent Arrow wasn't going to finish her sentence. His chest rumbled, hand running up the length of Arrow's spine. "That we are all evil? And like to eat fairies?"

Arrow bit her lip and nodded slowly, still too scared to say anything.

Val snorted and shook his head. "A nasty rumor started over a century ago when our cities split. On the contrary, I particularly like fairies. And I really like the one sitting on my lap right now. Even though, in hindsight, I should have told you what I was from the start."

Arrow peeked a glance at Val's face. His eyes were still closed, head leaning back against the bed frame. "Were you scared I would run away if you did?" Arrow whispered, and Val smiled softly.

"I was more thinking along the lines of how lucky I was that the prettiest fairy in all the lands somehow landed on my couch."

VALENTINE'S ARROW

Arrow tsked and smacked Val on the chest. "Oh, stop it."

Val rumbled and cracked an eye open. "Stop what, Princess? Stating facts?"

Arrow giggled as her panic melted away, and she turned in Val's arms. "So, you aren't going to turn me into fairy mince meat and gobble me up?"

Val shifted, hand running down Arrow's thigh. He pulled at her legs, and she ended up straddling him. "I never said that," he purred.

Arrow blushed as Val moved his way flat on the bed and pushed her farther up in the process. She gasped as his hot breath grazed her inner thighs and moved to grab the headboard. His hands massaged her ass as his tongue danced wickedly across her pussy. Arrow groaned in pleasure, and she closed her eyes. Her hands fell from the headboard, weaving through Val's silky hair as her hips took on a life of their own.

She rode Val's face as their groans of pleasure filled the silent room. Much too soon, Arrow felt the heat building within her explode outward as she came. A shiver slid down her spine as Val gave Arrow one last lick before letting her slide off his face. He scooped her limp body into his arms and tapped her nose gently. Arrow gave Val a lazy smile, "I stand corrected. Maybe I do want to be gobbled up by the big bad Hell Cat."

Val laughed. "Come now, Princess. Let's shower and maybe this big bad Hell Cat will make you something for breakfast."

Chapter Six

Arrow munched on an apple slice as Val rolled his eyes, listening to the other person ramble over the phone.

"Fine, I'll be there in twenty minutes." He hung up with a curse and glanced at Arrow. She fought a blush as her entire body simmered from his gaze. He reached out, ruffling her semi dry hair. "Princess, I have to go to work. Promise not to run away while I'm gone?"

Arrow smiled. "And what would happen if I ran away?"

Val purred, eyes hooding as he leaned into her space, his lips scrapping against hers. "I would just have to chase after you."

Arrow lost the fight and felt her face turn red at the thought, her breathing already going shallow. She groaned in displeasure as Val leaned away and straightened his tie. Arrow had to admit, he looked spectacular in a suit. It did nothing to mask his gorgeous frame. Quite the opposite. It emphasized every delicious part of him.

He blew her a kiss before stalking out the door and Arrow sighed. She spun the chair she was in and almost fell off in fright as she came face to face with Desi, back in human form. Her hand flew to her chest, heart beating a mile a minute. "Desi, you startled me."

Desi smiled and pushed the party planner book in Arrow's direction. "Now you are mine for the day," she purred with absolute glee.

Arrow narrowed her eyes, but didn't say anything as she pulled the planner closer and started thumbing through it. About twenty minutes later, Arrow slammed the planner shut and glared at Desi. "Why are you staring at me like that?"

Desi grinned widely, showing off her pearly white teeth. She propped her chin on her hand and a dreamy look overtook her face. "I'm just happy."

Arrow rolled her eyes. "Let's just concentrate on the event you want me to help plan. You have some good ideas in here, but I need to know more about the city and what will attract people to sign up on such short notice."

Desi snapped to attention, giving Arrow a mock salute, "Yes, ma'am. Well... first, a real-life fairy will attract attention. So that's a plus."

Arrow frowned and shook her head. "I am so in the dark about this city. No pun intended. But if the citizens here want to see a real-life fairy, they could just take a trip to Fairy City."

Desi frowned and shook her head. "There are still a lot of misconceptions about the people and creatures here in the Night City. Most people don't go to your city because we don't want to cause a scene or scare you all."

"Oh... I, I guess you are correct. I mean..." Arrow blushed. "I had the same misconception. But I am beginning to see I was wrong."

Desi snorted and shook her head. "Oh! That reminds me. I forgot to ask. What even made you come this way?"

Arrow blushed and glanced away. She placed her hands in her lap gently, "Well... I got into a little trouble with the law and got fired because of it."

"What for?" Desi whispered and leaned in close as if Arrow were hiding a secret.

Arrow shook her head. "It was just something stupid. My ex and his friends were involved. It was an accident and my hair kind of caught on fire.

But you know that wasn't what pushed me over the edge. He cheated on me. Because I wasn't pretty without long hair and I kind of lost it. I trashed his apartment, and he threatened to report me. Then all I remember is absolute anger raging through me. Next thing I know, my ex's wings are glued together, and I was arrested." Arrow finally took a breath and glanced at Desi. Her eyes had turned cold, silver fire flickering within. "Uhhhh..." Arrow faltered as a bit of steam snuck out of Desi's nose.

"I'll kill them. Just point me in their direction, and I'll—"

Arrow reached over quickly and squeezed Desi's hand. "I already took care of it. Hence getting fired and not being able to find a job in Fairy City. But it's fine. This incident wouldn't have pushed me to take a chance in coming here. And I wouldn't have met you or Val."

Desi smiled and Arrow opened the planner once more. She stared at the pages without really reading them, an awkward silence building. She started slightly as Desi reached over and placed her hand over Arrow's.

"My brother really likes you," she whispered.

Arrow sighed. "Is it weird that I really like him too? But I can't explain why I'm so instantly infatuated with him. I just am."

Desi snorted and shook her head. "No, it isn't weird. It's actually quite normal. We are all a bunch of shifters and predators in this city. We see what we want and chase after it. Insta lust is sort of part of the territory. And most of the time, it is because you found your mate. Chalk it up to animal instinct."

Arrow bit her lip, mulling over Desi's words. She pushed a stray lock of hair behind her ear, heart going a mile a minute. "Do... do... you think..." Arrow couldn't finish her sentence and Desi shrugged.

"What I think doesn't matter, but I've never seen my brother act this way before. Usually, he is much more reserved and intimidating." Desi sat straight up and frowned, trying to imitate Val.

Arrow giggled and shook her head. "Enough nonsense and talk about your brother."

"And your lover," Desi quipped and Arrow snorted.

"As I was saying, enough nonsense. I think I have an idea about the event."

Arrow's comment perked Desi up, shifting her focus, and she leaned forward. Arrow shifted the planner around and pointed at two very different ideas.

"I think I know a way to combine these ideas seamlessly into one event."

Desi's eyes lit up and an impish smile overtook her face. "Now that... that sounds like a perfect idea."

Arrow smiled back. "Then let's get started."

Chapter Seven

Arrow buzzed about, flitting across the grassy overlook and between a gaggle of people. She greeted them and sprinkled sparkling fairy dust into the sky, eliciting happy claps and smiles.

Vampires, demons, and shifters of all kinds arrived in batches; the event already sold out. Arrow buzzed into the red and gold dropped tent, snatching more vials of the fairy dust, which was actually a mix of colored sugar and glitter. She was about to take flight again, but a large chest blocked her way and Arrow squealed, jumping into Val's arms.

"Princess," he purred and caught her mid leap. The kiss he gave Arrow scorched her down to the toes. She was breathless when Val pulled away and he chuckled before putting her back on the ground. "Princess," he purred again, this time glancing around the tent and everything beyond. "This is an amazing idea."

Arrow beamed from the praise. "It was actually you and Desi that gave me the idea. With all your chasing talk. Speaking of which…"

A couple emerged from the forest beyond with wolfish grins and wrinkled clothes. Arrow floated over and sprinkled some dust on them with a giggle before flying back to Val. They watched as the couple disappeared into the tent. The sounds of laughter and glasses tinkling warmed Arrow's heart. Desi emerged a few minutes later and headed over to Arrow and Val. She was bouncing from excitement, the plastic clipboard in her hands slightly cracked. Arrow snorted and snatched it away from her. She flipped through the list of names and checkmarks. "That was the last couple, right?"

Desi spun around and glanced at the sky. "It was, and just in time, too. Arrow, you are a freaking genius. I can't believe you set up a moonlit forest chase and a sunrise banquet. You timed it perfectly."

Arrow blushed and shook her head. "I wasn't that hard. I just liked both the ideas."

Desi laughed and glanced at Val. "Wasn't hard, she says. I'm pretty sure she hasn't slept in two days." She looked at Arrow. "You also look super tense."

Val gave Arrow a sideways glance and a grin that melted her panties off. "Hmmm... I can think of something that might relax her a bit. Since she has been so busy for the last two days."

Desi jumped up and down, "Yes! You two should take part in the forest chase." She turned toward Arrow. "You will have so much fun. I promise."

Arrow bit her lip, glancing to the sky, which was already lightening, and then to the drop tent. "Are you sure you can handle the sunrise banquet by yourself?"

Desi tsked and snatched the clipboard away from Arrow. "Pleaseeeee, I can totally handle it. Now go. Have some fun."

Arrow blushed and glanced over at Val and the forest behind them. "So do I just..." She motioned a hand toward the forest.

Val winked at her and loosened his tie. He pulled it over his head and kicked off his shoes at the same time. Arrow's eyes widened as a low growl rumbled from his chest. "Run, Princess."

Arrow didn't need to be told twice as she sprinted away and took flight. She stayed low, zigging and zagging through the trees. Excitement

VALENTINE'S ARROW

and adrenaline flooded through her veins as Val chased after her. Time blurred, only the excitement of being pursued filled her thoughts. She was in the middle of zagging around a tree branch when a powerful hand wrapped around her ankle and yanked Arrow out of the air.

She squeaked in surprise before laughing as Val's muscular arms wrapped around her. He toppled them to the soft forest floor and suddenly his lips were on hers. Heavy breathing mingled with moans, hands tearing at clothing. Val turned her around, hands at her hips angling her butt up while Arrow lowered her arms and chest to the ground. Val growled as he trailed a finger up her already slick entrance.

Her pussy throbbed for his touch and clenched as he slowly thrusted a finger inside. Arrow moaned and sank onto the ground lower, legs widening. The soft forest floor was damp against her bare knees, soft and forgiving unlike Val's cock, which was already demanding entrance into her wet folds. "Are you ready for me, Princess?"

"Yes, yes, please," Arrow pleaded as Val worked himself inside of her. The angle was deep, and Arrow moaned, gripping the forest floor beneath her fingertips. Her eyes rolled back, pussy throbbing. Heat pooled steadily inside until it spilled over, pussy clenching and releasing against Val's cock as he bottomed out inside of her. Fingers trailed up her spine and Val grabbed her gently on the back of the neck. His fingers wove into her hair, his other hand coming to the ground next to hers.

He was careful not to squish her wings between their bodies as he rode her. His thrusts slow and deep as Arrow's moans filled the morning air. Pleasure coiled through her again, making its way down her spine to the tips of her toes.

"Fuck, Princess. Keep moaning for me," Val rumbled as his cock got even harder inside of her.

Arrow felt him pick up speed and her orgasm spilled over once more as Val released inside of her. She collapsed to the forest floor, completely spent, her body riding a pleasure high.

Val bundled her in his arms and Arrow laid her head on his hard chest, listening to his rapid heartbeat intermingling with purring. Reaching over, Arrow interlaced her fingers with his. A smile blossomed on her face as Val lifted their clasped hand to his mouth and kissed her fingertips. "I missed you," he rumbled and Arrow giggled.

"I was only two days. Plus, you didn't even know me until four days ago."

Val nipped at her fingertips. "Doesn't matter, Princess. You're my favorite meal and I want it daily. I want to hear your moans of pleasure and feel you clenching around my cock like you can't get enough of me. Because I can't get enough of you."

VALENTINE'S ARROW

Arrow pushed away from Val's chest and straddled him. She leaned down and gave him a kiss, licked at his lips and murmured. "I'm your mate, aren't I?"

"Yes. I knew it the second Desi brought you into the house. But we can take it slow, Princess. I don't want to rush you."

Arrow scoffed and shook her head. She gave Val another kiss. "I don't want slow. I want you."

Val chuckled and wrapped his arms around her. "Good. Because you have me. Happy Valentine's Day, Princess."

"Happy Valentine's Day, my mate," Arrow whispered back and snuggled into the warm embrace of Val's arms to watch the sunrise on the happiest day of her life.

The End

Also by Astrid Vail

Get signed paperbacks at my website www.astridvail.com or find your next eBook in Kindle Unlimited
Wicked Fate, Lusty Mates

Enter a new world of desire with a coven of misfit witches and the steamy discovery of their lycanthrope mates in this brand new series.

Carnal Moon: A Steamy M/F Paranormal Erotic Romance

Wild Moon: A Smoldering M/F Paranormal Erotic Romance

Enchanted Moon: A Second Chance M/F Paranormal Erotic Romance

Arctic Moon: A Sultry M/F Paranormal Erotic Romance

Feral Moon – A Seductive M/F Paranormal Erotic Romance

Scarlet Moon – A Spicy M/F Paranormal Erotic Romance

Fairytales After Dark

Claiming Jafar: A M/F Enemies to Lovers 'Villain gets the Girl' Fairytale

Gaston's Beast: An Achillean Beauty and the Beast Retelling

Hunting Red: A Sapphic Red Riding Hood Reimagining

Princess Bound: A M/F Friends to Enemies to Lovers Steampunk Fairytale.

Wicked Snow: A 'Why Choose' Dark Romance Snow White Retelling

Holidays After Dark

Winter's Eve: A M/F Fantasy Holiday Short Story

Valentine's Arrow: A M/F Paranormal Holiday Short Story

Fireworks in the Bayou: A M/F Paranormal Holiday Short Story

Courting Sin

Courting Sin : A M/F Devilish Short Story Part One for newsletter subscribers only

Craving Sin: A M/F Devilish Short Story Part Two for newsletter subscribers only

About Astrid Vail

Wild Romance, Epic Adventure – Multi Genre Romance Author
Storyteller at Heart
Born in the backwoods of California, Astrid Vail was raised upon fairytales and fantasy worlds. With a love of everything otherworldly, Astrid decided to put pen to paper and pull the exotic creatures dancing in her head out into the light of day. She has been writing professionally since 2022 and has no intention of slowing down anytime soon. Signup to her newsletter at www.astridvail.com for a free book or two, cover reveals, and all things related to extra spicy book news.

Made in the USA
Columbia, SC
10 February 2025